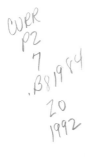

With thanks to Joseph
for his invaluable contribution — A.B.

This is a Borzoi Book published by Alfred A. Knopf, Inc.

Manufactured in Hong Kong   1   2   3   4   5   6   7   8   9   10

Library of Congress Cataloging-in-Publication Data
Browne, Anthony. Zoo / Anthony Browne.   p.   cm.
Summary: A boy endures a tedious visit to the zoo with his family.
ISBN 0-679-83946-1 (trade)   ISBN 0-679-93946-6 (lib. bdg.)
[1. Zoos—Fiction. 2. Zoo animals—Fiction.] I. Title.   PZ7.B81984Zo   1993   [E]—dc20   92-11708

ZOO

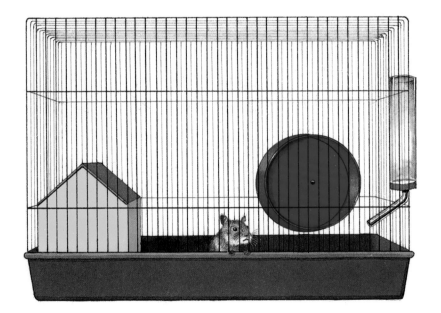

ANTHONY BROWNE

ALFRED A. KNOPF · NEW YORK

My Family

Me.

My brother.

Dad.

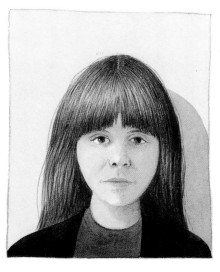

Mum.

Last Sunday we all went to the zoo.
Me and my brother were really excited.

But there were masses of cars on the road,
and it took ages to get there. After a while
Harry and I got really bored. So we had a
fight. Harry started crying and Dad told
me off. It's not fair, he never tells Harry
off. It's always *my* fault.

"What kind of jam do you get stuck in?"
asked Dad.

"Don't know," said Harry.

"A traffic jam!" roared Dad.

Everyone laughed except Mum and Harry
and me.

When we finally got there Dad *had* to
have a quarrel with the man in the ticket
booth. He tried to say that Harry was only
four and should get in half-price. (He's
five and a half, actually.)

"Highway robbery!" Dad snarled.
Sometimes he can be really embarrassing.

We hadn't gotten a map of the zoo, so we just
wandered around. Me and my brother wanted to
see the gorillas and monkeys, but we had to see
all these boring animals first. We went into the
elephant house, which was really smelly. The
elephant just stood in a corner stuffing its face.

Mum had brought some chocolate, and
Harry and I were starving. "Can we have
it now?" I asked.

   "No, not yet," said Dad.

   "Why not?" whined Harry.

   "Because," said Dad.

   "Because what?" I asked.

   "Because I say so," said Dad. It seemed
he was in one of his moods.

Then we saw the tigers. One of them was just walking along a wall of the cage, then turning around and walking all of the way back. Then it would start again.

"Poor thing," said Mum.

"You wouldn't say that if it was chasing after you," snorted Dad. "Look at those nasty teeth!"

Harry and I were getting really hungry.
"Can't we have lunch now?" I asked.
     "But we just got here," said Mum.
     It seemed like we'd been there for hours.
My brother thumped me, so I kicked him,
and we wrestled for a bit, then Dad told
me off.

We looked at the penguins next. I usually
find penguins funny when I see them on
TV, but all I could think of was food.

"What animal can you eat at the zoo?"
asked Dad.

"Don't know," I groaned.

"A hot dog!" howled Dad. He was holding
his stomach and laughing so much that
tears were rolling down his face.

"Come on, boys," said Mum. "Let's get
something to eat."

The café was great. I had a burger and fries and
baked beans and loads of ketchup, and a chocolate
ice cream with raspberry sauce. It was great.
    After that we went into the gift shop to spend
our pocket money. We each bought a funny
monkey hat. "Which one is the monkey?" jeered
you-know-who.

Then we had to go and see the polar bear.
It looked really stupid, just walking up and down,
up and down.

Next we saw the baboons, and they were a bit more interesting. Two of them had a fight. "They remind me of someone," said Mum. "I can't think who."

The orangutan crouched in a corner and didn't move.
We tried shouting at it and banging on the glass, but it
just ignored us. Miserable thing.

Finally we found the gorillas, they were quite good. Of course Dad had to do his King Kong impersonation, but luckily we were the only ones there.

Then it was time to go home. In the car Mum asked us what was the best part of the day. I said the burger and fries and beans, and Harry said the monkey hats.

Dad said the best part was going home, and asked her what was for dinner.

"I don't think the zoo really is for animals," said Mum. "I think it's for people."

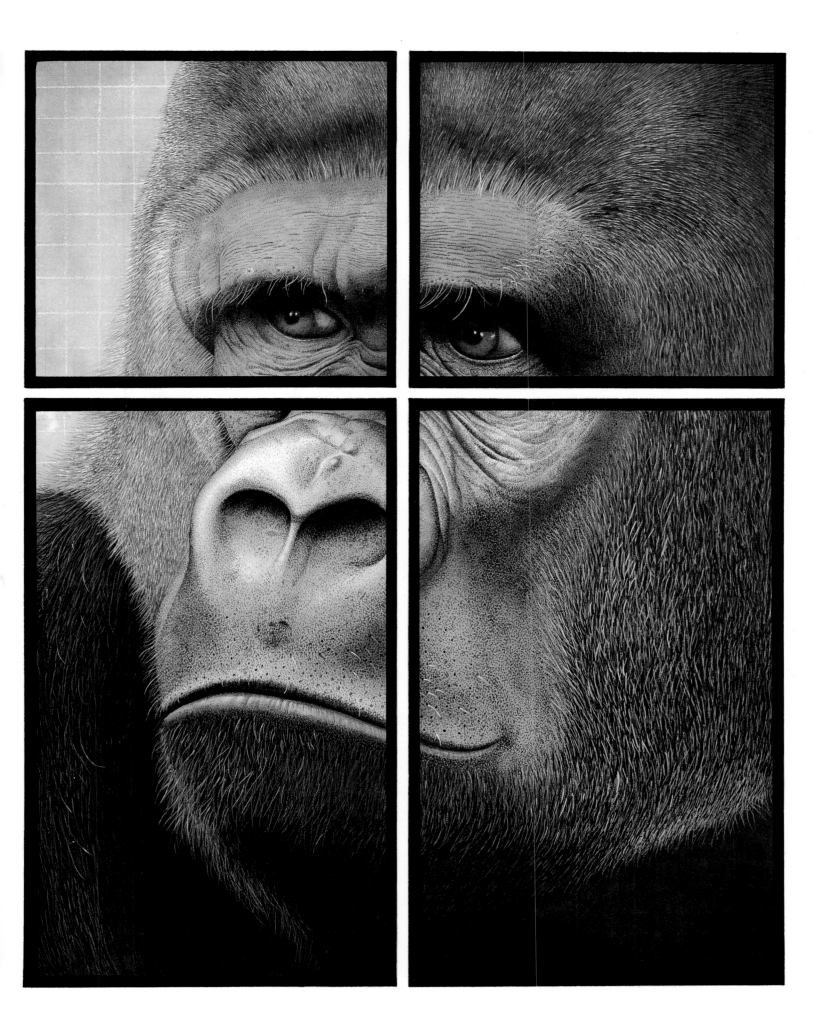

That night I had a very strange dream.

Do you think animals have dreams?